*The Better
to
See You*

The Better
to
See You

by
Alfonso Quijada Urías

translated by
Hugh Hazelton

Cormorant Books

Published with the assistance of the Canada Council and the Ontario Arts Council.

Originally published as *Para mirarte mejor* by Editorial Guaymuras, S.A., Tegucigalpa, Honduras, 1987.

Edited by Gena K. Gorrell.

Cover image from an oil on canvas, *Le Punk*, by Juan Wenceslao Zamora Castro, courtesy of the artist.

Cover design by Artcetera Graphics, Dunvegan, Ontario.

Published by Cormorant Books Inc.,
RR #1, Dunvegan, Ontario,
Canada K0C 1J0.

Printed and bound in Canada.

Canadian Cataloguing in Publication Data

Quijada Urías, Alfonso, 1940-
   The better to see you

Translaton of: Para mirarte mejor.
ISBN 0-920953-59-X

   1. El Salvador--Fiction. I. Title.

PS8583.U344P3713 1993   C861   C93-090538-5
PR9199.3.Q84P3713 1993

Contents

Washington, January 25. President Roosevelt has declared that when his term as president is over, he will visit Central America, where he will hunt tigers and elephants.

Diario del Salvador, 1906

. . . . and if I ceased to exist, all my memories would also cease to exist. Yes, he thought. Between sorrow and nothingness, I choose sorrow.

William Faulkner

"For Jesus God's sake, don't kill me."
"Don't mention God to us: we're animals," the sergeant said, and ordered a soldier to shoot him.

"Massacre in Sumpul",
El Tiempo, Honduras, 1980

In the Shadow of an Old Woman in Flower

A demented sun writhing like a snake in the orphaned, turbulent landscape. Noisy everyday crowd. The city besieged. The thousand eyes of the buildings watching. How long? The mute history of organized banality. State of siege. Siege of the lunatic state. Sirens of Ulysses, driver for the firemen. People walking hurriedly. Complaining about the heat and the squeeze of the sardine-buses. Mortified sensations of distrust. Fear of dying while walking along the streets of San Sivar. On Avenida de España or Delano Roosevelt. Dead breaths that I inhale to live. Bullets whistle. The guns are bleating. The mad sun gives off a sweaty heat. Broken down. The radio of the Flor de París shoe store turned up full blast: the national anthem in the background. A shadowy voice from a drainpipe announcing the state of siege. Every day must come to an end. Leaves on the rooftops. Crops of the sun. Coins flowering over the city. Clouds on the horizon. Flocks of black sheep along the cliff. Bleating. Hired mourners.

    That's the way things are here. Behind the apparent calm of the cafés. Behind that feigned stillness a whirlwind is rising. A pandemonium. And suddenly cars turn around. Go back the other way. Collide. Coil together. Run stoplights. Shots. Firing. Flight of terrified pigeons. Panicked. It's in San Miguelito, yells the real-estate salesman: they've hit the bank. All four are dead.

("Terrorists," *El Diablo de Hoy* will announce. Page one.) They found out later that one was a minister of the Latter-Day Saints. Another was carrying a Don Quixote brand notebook full of love poems. Celia heard the same story. The taxi driver told it to her with a wealth of detail. He'd been trapped. Sweating bricks on a corner in San Miguelito. The thousand and one stories that are told of that hellish day.

The same night. At nearly one hundred years of age, the mother of invention rising from eternity into eternity. She died. The bright ideas they get at her age: of dying ex-act-ly at that time. During those black days.

She died because she wanted to; she didn't like the world any more. This infernal, sordid world. She was the grandmother of the neighbourhood. Of the community. Of life. Was there anyone who didn't know her? She fought with rooster-tailed kids. She got drunk on weekends and holidays. An inordinate reader of Eugène Sue, Vargas Vila and Geneviève de Brabant. Played games like Viva la Flor, Who With? and Chinese checkers with astounding perfection. At times, when her feet got itchy and her head boiled with stubborn, obsessive ideas, she used to take off at a mule trot for the mountains of Honduras. She'd go there with her flowery chests filled with porcelain, magnetic stones, lace, patent-leather pumps, gold coins, mercerized cottons, pins, enchanted birds, books of poems, magic powders, prayer books. And a lot more that went into her most perfect of inventories.

That day. Every day must come to an end. We held her funeral. As decently as she had dreamed. Everyone was there. Congregated. Legendary family legions. Generations upon generations. The origin of their species. The most distant relatives. So far removed they seemed invisible. Innumerable. That whole universe speaking of her: the

—8—

great saintly woman. Without a navel. Irreproachable. Pure as a stomach of white parchment. As a vagina white as cauliflower.

What was the problem? The dilemma? Every death certificate requires a birth certificate. Travel papers. The record of her birth had been lost. Seed of her origin.

Later Adam recounted the story of everyone we had to consult: dignitaries, magistrates, ailing old folks. Cause a whole idiotic commotion; knock on countless doors; cross living rooms, impenetrable houses. Patios full of flowers and shining leaves. We sat down with doctors of law. Went to the great-great-grandfather himself. It took us a century to check up on it. Discover the original version. The great elder finally came up with the answer. Her name had been Cleotilde Barrios. Not Isadora Cartagena, the one she went under. She'd been born in 1899 in the La Vega neighbourhood. "Whose personal details had been given by the child's father in the presence of the municipal secretary." Who had signed the present document.

After that mix-up came the problem of the burial. Which proved to be far more complex. Because it involved crossing the city in wartime. We had to risk it. Of course. Waves of war were crashing against the walls of the Sisters of Charity. The still trees, leaves green like translucent jade. Nothing moves unless He wills it. We had to give her a Christian burial. Dare to make the difficult pilgrimage. Go up Arce Street. Cross Avenida de España. Turn onto Darío. Come out on El Calvario; then straight down to the General Cemetery. And finally bury her. Yes. With all due urgency. Give her the most Christian burial possible in these times of war. Apocalyptic sadness. Trumpets of Jericho. Wailing Wall. My God.

So there we go. Behind the hearse. Black. Solemn. How serious are the dead and those who bury them. The people from the funeral parlour. The little man in the black suit with his accounting notebook. The driver and his tiny goatee. And those peculiar smells: a reek of death and irises. Cologne. Chemical decomposition of the body. Funeral wreaths. Somewhere between the fragrance of life and that of death. Our remembering. Ceremoniously thoughtful: those days of our elder mother. Remembering the hour when she would drink her "sugarcane spirits". Her elixir of life. And sing. And swear at everyone. She advised her daughters to quit being so squeamish about their virginity. And one thing and another. At night she used to talk about her former adventures. Her stories of when she joined General Mendieta's forces as a camp follower. In '26. Or about her countless love affairs. Leading back to the pure fountain. The original patio. The cosmic return of the Great Mother. And we saw her once again in scenes like the day she came home from the war in Honduras loaded with booty. Two trucks full of liquor. Four juke-boxes. Three ice makers. Two bars. Five living-room suites. Six dining-room sets. Two billiard tables. And more than enough knick-knacks to fill up any accounting notebook. All those things. That beautiful day we went out to meet her. Thrilled. Patriotic. The endless party that followed. Six weeks of non-stop musical bedlam. Night and day. Day and night.

Listen, I told the driver, try not to go through downtown. There's always a bunch of them down by the post office. But the little know-it-all's only reaction was to twitch his miniature goatee. Look, I insisted, let's not get in a jam. We're better off taking one of the side streets that run into Plazuela Barrios or de la Policía. But the guy went straight on. With the same wooden expression. Indolent. As if nothing could go wrong.

So we moved along at a tortoise pace. Through

that peaceful downtown area. Following the black car. With forebodings of trouble. We passed Arce, Plaza San José, the used-book stalls. Shoeshine guys. Pigeons. The whiteness of flocks of pigeons cleansing the hot, dirty four-o'clock air. Cold-drink and ice-cream stalls. Schoolgirls in blue and white. Their faces made up like the models in the last issue of *Vanidades*. Tigresses and vampires. Little personalities. The lady with elephantiasis sitting in front of the General Electric building. And farther on, drunks and tourists coming out of Chico's Bar and the New World Hotel. Old bars of past binges. Then. At that moment. The hornet's nest broke loose. Like the thunder of the sea. People panicking. Sirens and gunfire. Cars started turning around. Skidding sideways. Crashing into each other. Stalling. Lurching forward. Screams. Doors closing. That's how the tumult started. Gunshots followed by fear. Everyone began running. Jumping. Looking for a way out. Some place safe, as the heavy steel blinds came down over the bakeries, grocery stores, cafés. Because after the firing and the turmoil came a swarm of people. Pillaging. Wild-eyed. Dissolute. "Another student massacre." The ones who took over the cathedral, yells a terrified woman. Monsignor has just come out. Everything's red. Blood-red. And evenings and flowers. Blood of our blood. Those who were massacred will be avenged. The Río Lempa stained with blood one thousand nine hundred and thirty-two times over. Stairways covered with blood, skin. Brains. A new funeral pyramid.

In the distance. Scattered spots. Crowds like heads of pins. Suspension (. . .) marks running helter-skelter. Through the smoke and ashen gleam of afternoon. A bus engulfed in flames on the corner of Dragón.

Despite all those incidents. The old astute logic of the fox. We escaped danger. The labyrinth. The wild confusion. The slaughter. Far from the zone of fire. Making our way through. Drawing back. Moving forward. We sank into alleys. Ancient passageways. Large ramshackle houses. Old places in an anonymous San Salvador. Primitive. Remnants of a railway. Carts. Mule stalls. Ancient solemn barbershops with names like "La Francesita" and "Fígaro Sí". Slipping away down bends in the road. Finally we arrived at the cemetery. Dispersed. Downhearted. At the main gate from different directions. All of us. Except the hearse. Except the remains of the one who was no longer alive. The ironies of life.

There at last. Nervous. One cigarette after another, we got hold of the thread of the thing. The thread of Ariadne. Whaddyagonnado. We waited for everyone to calm down enough to help look for the coffin. The lost ark. Urn of our empress.

Other stories began to circulate. No less outlandish. Had the hearse been crushed by one of those gigantic sardine-buses? Or the driver been picked up for acting suspicious? Along with the car and all? Opinions sprang up. Among the more desperate: we should call the Red Cross or the fire department. Another one: buy an ad on Radio KL asking for information as to the whereabouts of a magnificent hearse. A '66 Chevrolet. Four-door. Licence 26000. With the mortal remains of Cleotilde Barrios. Generally known as The Bandit.

But it was all in vain. Vanity of vanities. While we were thinking and rethinking what to do, shadows were falling. Like a Chinese painting. Inkblots over the white mausoleums. Over the tombs. Over the dark earth. And as they were closing the gate. The creak of plaintive doors. The funeral car appeared around the corner. Twice as black. Sepulchral. And then an absurd rejoicing with hurrays and *vivas*. Followed by a gloomy amazement.

Black spring.

We had to get her buried quickly. To leave her once and for all in the peace or war of her holy sepulchre. Tears. Seas of weeping. Gnashing of teeth. Sighs. Faintings. Tachycardia. We had to pay the ill-fated little man. And the custodian who had refused to open— regulations in hand—that portentous gate. We swore frenetically at the obstinate driver and were on the point of lynching him for having put us through this mess. Then. At last. The gaunt little guard gave in and reopened the huge gate.

Leaping. Almost falling flat over the tombs and mausoleums, we finally found her gravesite. Empty and round like an O. Like the mouth of nothingness. A mouthful. Holding the cords. Letting the varnished casket slip down. Coffer of what had been. Into the depths of the earth. The creak of the wood. We left her there. Her remains deposited in the dark kingdom of eternity. Then came the earth. Spongy. Falling hard and heavily. Loosely and darkly onto the glass and wood. Making a muffled noise. Like a drum. The lugubrious drum that bids farewell to the dead. The tom-tom of death. And once more of course oceans of weeping. Hurricanes of sighs. Forests of cries and lamentations.

At last. Every day must come to an end. The funerary casket remained lost in the funereal kingdom. Sealed beneath a thousand and more coverings of earth. Far beneath. Compressed by the earth. Which was hard. Compact. Black. We were in a great rush to bury her. A very great rush. Before the night got any darker.

When we got home the mother was there. Behind the curtains. In her wicker rocking-chair. With a glass of sugarcane spirits in her hand. Rocking herself. As if nothing had happened. As if nothing had happened.

Downhill Night

A light shower spattered the city. The wipers squeaked over the grimy windshield. There were a lot of clothes hanging outside the stores, and the breeze stirred the handkerchiefs and shirts; flocks of pigeons flew restlessly over the roof of the National Palace. The Datsun plunged forward, coughing out of its broken muffler. The street was empty. At that hour it was always empty. At the corner of the Palace, a woman was selling gum and cigarettes while holding a broken umbrella in one hand and a cup of coffee in the other.

"Tell the old girl to give you a pack of Deltas," said the Gorilla to Softy as he slowed down.

Softy opened the car window and pointed out the cigarettes to the woman with a one-peso note.

She brought him the cigarettes and his change.

The Gorilla accelerated.

"What d'ya wanta do today?" he asked.

"Have a few drinks, I guess," Softy answered. "With all this drizzle, it'd be just the thing to get your motor working."

"How about gettin' into some of that whisky we confiscated from the gringo?" the Gorilla suggested.

"Good idea," said Softy, "but it's in the—"

"No it isn't," interrupted the Gorilla. "I already had a taste of it. I knew my guts would be begging for it about this time of day. Get it out from under the seat."

"You're ready for everything," said Softy, reaching for the bottle of Special Blend. "Now let's find a place to drink it."

"What d'ya say to El Cuzcatlán?" the Gorilla asked him. "The old lady down there'll treat us like kings. . . ."

"Let's give it a shot."

The Gorilla nodded, turned left and accelerated up the street. The car left a trail of dense black smoke.

"We got till eight-thirty," said Softy, "and it's just after six."

"That gives us plenty'a time," said the Gorilla. "A coupla stiff ones and then back on the road. I hope things work out tonight."

"They will," said Softy, "with a little luck. Here we are." He opened the car door. "This old baby still hauls ass, doesn't it?"

"Even with a dirty carburetor," said the Gorilla, getting out and putting his pistol in his belt.

"What's new, Big Mama?" asked Softy as he came in.

"Just what you see," said Big Mama; "always ready to serve the clientele."

"That's the way I like it," said the Gorilla, shaking hands with her and heading for a table. "That's why we came; spots like this are gettin' to be relics now."

"Other places are more modern," said Softy, "but what with the attention you get here and the tasteful—"

"That's what my clients tell me," Big Mama broke in. "Have a seat and—Matilda! Take care of these two gentlemen, pleeease."

"Thanks," said the Gorilla. "We brought some whisky."

"I take it with a little Coke," said Softy, "and if

you've got any snacks—"

"I'll have mine with ginger ale and ice," said the Gorilla.

"Make yourself at home," said Big Mama, and she called out again, "Matilda, see to these gentlemen right away, please."

"Not many customers here today," Softy remarked.

"No," Big Mama answered, "business is going from bad to worse. People are afraid, they don't want to go out any more after what happened at the—"

"Yep. That's the way it is," interrupted the Gorilla, "but you got nothing to be afraid of so long as you're a friend of authority and live close to the law."

"That's how I like it, Matilda baby," said Softy, putting his arms around the girl who brought glasses and soft drinks over to their table. "One of these days I'll take you out for a spin and—"

"Hey!" Matilda burst out. "You know I've got a husband!"

"So what?" said Softy. "I'll take 'em any old way, husbands and all!"

"Already gettin' carried away," said the Gorilla, "and you haven't even had your first drink yet."

"It's just that pussy makes me wild," said Softy, pouring a double shot of whisky into the Gorilla's glass. "Hey, Big Mama! Can I play a tune on the jukebox?"

"Go right ahead," said Big Mama. "If it's turned off, it's just that we didn't expect any customers. Margarita, switch on the jukebox for the gentlemen."

"And where'd this little Margarita come from?" asked the Gorilla, watching the girl's bottom out of the corner of his eye as he pressed a button for a song.

"She fell out of the sky," said Margarita, laughing.

"Like the Virgin Herself," said the Gorilla, "though she don't have nothin' on you," and he gave her a slap on the rear.

"Hey! This gentleman's gettin' out of line," complained Margarita. "He doesn't even respect the Church."

"This song's for you," said the Gorilla, just as "Caramba, Doña Lionor" started up on the jukebox, and the girl went back towards the kitchen, wiggling her hips.

"You're slowin' down," Softy told him. "I'm on my second drink already and you've barely—"

"So fuckin' what?" the Gorilla retorted. "Better late than never," and he knocked back his whisky.

"Big Mama's always on the lookout for tail," Softy noted.

"The right girls for the job," answered the Gorilla contentedly, serving himself another drink.

"This whisky's good stuff," Softy said, savouring his glass. "It's already warmin' up my brain."

"And you've only had two," replied the Gorilla. "Wait till we finish it off."

"Shit," said Softy, "it's so good to have a quiet drink. Too bad we still got that job to do at the—"

"No, it's better like this," mused the Gorilla. "Things turn out better when you're hammered; you'll see."

"Yeah," said Softy; "I guess you're right. It's not the same as doin' it cold, like the time we had to make that goddamn little teacher talk, the one Eyebrows got mixed up with Cayetano."

"You overdid it that time, man. You got nervous, and there's no sense rushin' the thing. You know it's a delicate job."

"It sure is," said Softy. "Comes with experience, I guess. You've sure as hell got a lot of self-control and willpower."

"I learned it from Eyebrows," said the Gorilla. "It's not for nothin' they call him a surgeon. He's got a delicate touch; no one almost ever dies on him."

"You know," Softy reflected, "Big Mama's still good for a screw—"

"If you don't mind dyin' in bed," replied the Gorilla, bursting out laughing.

"Hey baby, bring us another ginger ale!" Softy called to Margarita.

"Sure," said the girl, "but keep your hands off."

"Hey! Watch it over there," scolded Big Mama. "This is a decent place."

"You'd think it was a convent," croaked Softy mockingly.

"Hold on; Big Mama's gettin' mad," observed the Gorilla, as he tried to put his hand up the back of the girl's blouse.

"Yeck! This one's a real sleaze," Margarita exclaimed, dodging away from the Gorilla and quickly setting the ginger ale on the table.

"Big Mama's gettin' touchy," commented Softy.

"Real touchy," agreed the Gorilla.

"Watch out," said Softy; "don't forget she's got connections."

"I don't give a fuck," answered the Gorilla. "I'm not buggin' her, and anyway it's her fault for bringin' in ass like that."

"The next round's for the road," Softy proposed. "Let's not push our luck. We still got half an hour left."

"Damn," said the Gorilla, "time slips right away with this whisky. Seems like we just came in and—"

"Yep," replied Softy, "between liquor and pussy, the hours just fly."

"You said it," said the Gorilla, heading for the jukebox again.

"Shit," said Softy, following him, "I do believe Margarita really got to you."

"What the hell d'ya expect?" answered the Gorilla angrily, as "Caramba Doña Lionor" played for the tenth time.

"We'd better go," suggested Softy. "Duty first." He took the Gorilla by the arm and dragged him over to the bar.

"The bill, Big Mama," called out the Gorilla, "and please forgive any indiscretions; you understand we gotta have a little fun."

"Yeah," Softy added, "you know we're all right even if we sometimes—"

"Three-fifty," said Big Mama in a serious, drowsy voice.

"See ya later then," the Gorilla said. "And take care of the girls for me, 'cause sometime soon I'll—"

"Good night," replied Big Mama, annoyed, as she held out her hand with the change.

Outside the mist was rising up towards the trees and rooftops. The rain continued intermittently. There was the sound of car doors opening and shutting again and then the loud acceleration of the Datsun as it hurtled off down the deserted highway.

The Gorilla lit up a Delta. "We'll go back there another time," he said. "That dark little Margarita's gonna find out what's what. If the money's good, the girls never are," and he pushed the accelerator to the floor.

"It's eight-thirty," Softy remarked, pressing the light on his watch. "Have a drink," he added, passing the bottle to the Gorilla. "There's still a few shots left. Whaddya say we—"

"Let's drink her straight up," suggested the Gorilla, "so fast we never even taste it."

Softy opened the bottle, took a long swig and passed it to the Gorilla, who prescribed a similar dose for himself.

"Listen," the Gorilla told him, "maybe we better put off the whole operation till tomorrow. I don't feel up to it today."

"All right, whatever you say. You know there's no problem as far as I'm concerned."

"What we can do," the Gorilla proposed, "is just drive around a bit first."

"As usual," said Softy. "Nothing lost, and it gives us something to fill up the report with."

"Whaddya say we take a few minutes to check out the Colonia Centroamérica?" asked the Gorilla.

"Sounds good to me," declared Softy, taking another drink and passing the bottle back to the Gor.

"Now I'm really ready," said the Gorilla, taking out his pistol and putting it between his legs.

"The more shit-faced I get," said Softy, "the better my aim."

"Me too," added the Gorilla, turning off onto the main street of the Centroamérica neighbourhood.

"Better take her slow around here," advised Softy, as the noise from the motor died down.

"It don't matter," said the Gorilla. "They're lyin' low today, what with those teachers who ended up flat on their asses."

"Look," said Softy, pointing to a group of five teenagers, "there're the bastards now, always damaging private proper—"

"Let's not draw their attention," warned the Gorilla. "We'll go up and turn around at the end of the block while we get the hardware ready."

The Datsun continued on up the road, rounded the corner, turned and came back down the street again.

The boys, sensing a trap, began to run, their paint cans still in their hands. The one who'd been painting "Revolution or Dea—" left the message unfinished and fled with the others.

Softy aimed and got off the first shots, while the Gor braked sharply and nervously grabbed his gun.

Three of the boys, probably the lookouts, managed to jump over a wall; the other two kept running down the street.

"Leave those little bastards to me," said the Gorilla, stepping out of the car. "Watch me eat 'em up."

"Let's take one each," said Softy as he got out.

Together they pulled their triggers and, as the bullets hit home, the bodies were thrown forward and fell headlong onto the pavement. One of them lay bleeding into the mud with his head ripped open; the other sprawled with his face to the sky and bullet-holes across his chest.

"Good shootin'," said Softy, getting back into the car.

"Let's go," answered the Gorilla, his foot already on the accelerator, "before there's trouble."

"Step on it," said Softy, putting away his gun.

The cough of the Datsun went off down the street until it was lost among the other noises of the city.

Around the dead boys, like people looking over the edge of a deep well, a crowd began to form.

Mother Courage

There were four of the bastards, Chon my girl, like the four that came looking for Víctor Ardón, the guy who used to play piano in that group Larreynaga and then was never heard from again. They drove up in an old jalopy that was noisier than hell. It was late at night: musta been past twelve. You could hear everything: them shutting off the motor and gettin' outa the car, their footsteps heavy on the sidewalk outside and the clinking of their guns against their belt buckles—everything.

What happened was, they got into the house—I still don't know how—maybe over the mud wall behind Renderos's forge. Anyway, they forced the door, Chon girl, but then that must not've been too hard, since it was only fastened with a bit of cactus cord and held shut by a stool, just enough for me to keep those mangy cats out, and Rosa had only gotten home from her evening shift at the factory a few minutes before, and was so tired that the poor kid didn't even want to eat supper and went straight to bed.

I jumped up and saw the bastards and they lit up my face with their flashlights and hit me, slamming me up against the wall, and put a rifle to my chest.

"It's not the old lady we want," said the pug-nosed guy, the ugliest one of the gang; "it's the little terrorist bitch over there," and he pointed to poor Rosita, who was so tired and worn out she couldn't figure out what was going on.

"What're you talking about?" I told them, my fear actually making me brave. "She's a decent, hard-working girl."

"Yeah? That's why we're taking her," said the pug-nosed guy, putting his revolver to her head.

"Oh no you aren't," I told them. I was in a rage now. "You're not taking Rosita because if you do you'll defile her like you did all the others. You might as well just kill her right here in front of me, so I'll never have the pain of knowing you ruined her honour."

"Whatever the old bag wants," said the pug-nosed guy. "Make her happy," he told one of them, who was so drunk he could hardly stand up.

The man's arm was trembling, Chon girl, and I still didn't think the bastards were capable of doing it, but suddenly the guy with the shaking hands put his pistol up to Rosita's chest and fired—and I hear the noise and see her fall onto the baskets, her face unbelieving like it was all a bad dream, but then I see those guys walk out the door as cynical as can be and get back in that old wreck and drive off as if nothing had happened. And I'm there alone in the room, Chon girl, all alone, no one else around at that hour, with my daughter dead. And you've seen how I've been since then, Chon my girl: ever since that day I simply haven't wanted to go on living.

It's just too much for somebody my age to take, you know, Chon girl? It's just too much to take, isn't it?

Atlantis

Twenty years without seeing Sofía, since that night we went down to the Columbus Bridge, abandoning ourselves in an almost childish indifference. The turbulent river twisted like a snake through the purslane and haystacks and gave off a penetrating odour of sugarcane tops patiently chewed by herds of oxen, a smell of stalls and semen. And that morning twenty years later, Sofía suddenly reappeared, opening the door of the house next-door, and though fatter and older, she was still the same Sofía, with the same dark, melancholy eyes. Behind her loomed several pieces of dark furniture, a refrigerator, a radio and, in the background, lit by a soft glow, three little girls running around. We exchanged a spurious, dissembling look. I thought that perhaps she hadn't recognized me, which would have been better. By one of life's coincidences, we'd moved our printing shop into the house directly across from hers the week before.

We'd set up there with all our machinery, the strangest and most diverse apparatuses a printer's workshop ever had: a camera obscura, a Multilith printer, two drafting tables and an ancient desk with a model 69 Olivetti typewriter. And a lot of other things, too, which I won't go into now.

One afternoon Gonzalo came over to give us a detailed explanation of the inner workings of agitprop. Terezón got out the bills and receipts; he told him about the rise in the price of paper and ink, as well as the problems we'd been having with the old Multilith, for which it was almost impossible to get spare parts. It was a model from somewhere around Gutenberg's time; a police chief had stolen it during a raid on print shops suspected of putting out clandestine propaganda and had then resold it. Meanwhile we all drank coffee and retold the same old stories, that gradually wear out and become meaningless from being repeated too often.

We went on like that, adjusting, improvising, making plans that invariably went awry. Our surroundings, besides being gloomy, were sublimely absurd; nevertheless, that was where the idea of Atlantis Publishers first began to take form. Right next to our shop was an enormous shed that disgorged dozens of hot-dog carts from the Fantastic Bakery every morning, to the accompaniment of insults, noise, bolero tunes, squabbles and general commotion. The uniformed vendors in their mustard-coloured hats and red shirts always stopped to look in with surprise at our ancient machinery, as if we were working with prehistoric beasts. You could hear them whispering. The security guard would take his post at the door of the building and surreptitiously begin slicing his bread while a throng of feet tramped up and down the narrow stairs above.

In the shop, Guayo and the Moustache would pile up the paper at the same time every day, while Terezón washed the rollers, diligently squeezing them dry over and over again until they turned white. The paper always seemed to be of the worst possible quality, real junk; it was never any good for printing, even for the straight jobs we did during the day, and at night we'd often only be able to run off half the copies needed for the clandestine morning edition. After dark we worked with patience, in spite of our fear, for we were well aware of the dangers involved. We anticipated the risks and at times our skin crawled with the physical presence of our pursuers, with the torturers' shadowy hands. The air that came through our windows was stale, dead, filled with a moribund stench. The paper stuck to the rollers; we'd end up with more scrap than printed pages. The others would come by at two in the morning to pick up the first edition. The noise of the presses could be heard reverberating through the night, and whenever the machinery got stuck, the night watchman could be heard making his rounds, cracking the conspiratorial silence with his heels.

And you, where are you now, my heart, my love? Asleep without knowing, without guessing, that death could be laying its putrid egg this very night. Without knowing that I'm here uselessly imagining the day, assaulting the other side of reality, to create a new way of life. Isn't it true, my love? And I think of you asleep between the sheets, my flower of Lilliput.

Guayo would laugh nervously and Terezón would give me a slap on the back because of something I'd said. His shadow on the wall accentuated his Indian features: tough, intelligent, frank. We would open up another garbage bag: there was never enough room for those piles of inkstained papers, that mass of stained, letter-covered misprints. We were building a great brain out of bad copies.

"Look, we'd better stop this shit. It's almost two in the morning and we don't have fuck-all," the Moustache pointed out in a resigned voice.

"We go on until the paper runs out," said Terezón. A car could be heard chugging noisily down the North Road.

"Maybe it's them," said Guayo, scratching his head.

We went outside. The freshness of the night fell

over us like a net of infinite proportions. Far away, a rooster crowed, wounding the quiet solitude of the shadows. We walked out to the road. The car was there waiting. A door opened and Gonzalo appeared, enormous and heavy; the chassis lurched upward as he stepped out.

"The fucking machinery's done it again. Throw in the bloody paper, which is a dead loss," Terezón told him, "and all we managed to print was six thousand."

"Better than nothing," Gonzalo replied. "Close the damned place up and go get some sleep."

We spent the night at Moustache's house. In the morning we were awoken by a muffled noise. An earth tremor had made a bedroom wall collapse. Startled, we got up, made some coffee and started back to Atlantis. It was raining softly and slowly.

In those days, it always seemed that as soon as we got home, it was time to go back to work again. We were forever watching the same loop of film, except that away from work it was in living colour, without the hidden black-and-white fear it had at night. Reality this time. The rural landscape, transformed by winter—that green landscape of palm trees, hills, huts and country girls waving as you go past—is still back there in my memory, though now submerged by cars, crowds and dead-end streets: the city, the shock. On a corner in San Salvador a newsboy, dripping wet from a rainstorm, with a jute sack for a cape, was shouting out the headline of *La Prensa*: "Terrorist Band Uncovered." You gave him thirty centavos and began to leaf through the paper, and saw the photos of Rafa, Nico and Waldo. The Planning Headquarters. At that moment you suddenly, absurdly remembered a song by Pink Floyd. And you thought about what the butchers must be doing to the people in the photos. Ah! That was the line from the song. When will your turn come, Lamb of God? Your throat slit open in a cell by the glorious National Guard.

A huge demonstration was coming down Avenida España, filled with colours, pictures, paintings, signs, wild clothes, flowers, skins. It was made up of kids, young girls, students, workers, people from the slums, the fringes. There was your old nursemaid, the colour of a medlar tree, walking in the middle of the street. There was Andresito from the cane fields, and Miss Matilda, the chemistry professor. There were you, girl, my little bird, my pine flower, my tiny lizard, my amulet. There were you, Angelita Gómez, coming out of the Institute with that multicoloured hummingbird print on your shirt. There you were. There were all the protagonists of history. There were all those who never tired of shouting, of stirring things up. Of undermining.

At that moment we arrived—without noticing it—at Atlantis, resolved to carry on.

There you are once again, Sofía, grandmother of God. Sofía. And you're looking at me with eyes filled with suspicion. With that secret look, accusing me of getting involved in strange goings-on. What did you say? But your daughters look so much like you. The oldest, above all, brings back memories of that afternoon under the climbing vines. You rocked yourself back and forth, back and forth, in that squeaky rocking-chair, softly and crazily flowering towards the present time of life. And now. You appear in my path again. Your golden youth is gone, although you pretend to hold onto it through dresses and strange, intoxicating perfumes that you bring back from your trips abroad, and from the uncomfortable comfort you must feel in being Mrs. Santín—what an irony—the wife of the son of General Santín. I know you're watching me through the cracks, examining me. I know you're sure now that you've discovered who I am. I know by the way you walk, by your cloying gestures as you kiss and caress your daughters. By your innocent indifference. I know.

"All we need now is for the electricity to go on the fritz," said the Moustache, "just as we're setting up the plates."

"We've got to print before the night watchman comes by," Guayo contended.

"Let's do it, then," said Terezón. And the press began to turn. The pages were coming out clean, well-inked; the goddamn machine was doing wonderfully and the paper wasn't getting stuck. It was coming out softly ironed, smooth as snakeskin. Everyone, satisfied at last, was piling up pages. The printing was turning out incredibly well. Terezón was smiling delightedly. He looked like The Man Who Laughed, from that novel by Victor Hugo that Guayo was reading and would tell us about in his free time. The machine had finally found its own rhythm, its own music.

Later we heard the carts of the Fantastic Bakery starting to load up next door, and the little men in the mustard- and tomato-coloured suits began to file by like visitors from another planet. A smell of rotten cabbage came in on the morning air. Their faces were sad (with a sickly sadness), hungry, weatherbeaten. Beaten by the fists of an inclement life. Crushed.

"We've earned our daily bread," said the Moustache.

"Thanks to the celestial presses," said Guayo, smiling and pointing to our infernal machine.

"So let's have a bite," said Terezón, taking out some bread and refried beans from his Lintorrey bag.

That was when you appeared like a cinnamon flower and surprised me as I nibbled my cheese sandwich. All I saw was you, "jasmine in your hair and roses in your cheeks," and it was like returning to the last afternoon of that year long ago.

If that oaf of a husband of yours hadn't spoken to you, I wouldn't have stopped looking. I know that your eyes were scouring my face and body, searching for some clue, nook by nook, corner by corner. There wasn't a single spot your eyes didn't travel over, like dogs in a field of partridges.

Then came the matter of delivery: the delivery date, price and absolute necessity of getting out a set of business cards "by the 26th at the latest."

It grew quiet. Silence like an accomplice. You pretended not to know me, even when you went out saying good-afternoon-excuse-me. And you left just as a fine rain began to fall quietly on the rooftops and streets of the old part of the city. Even the taste of bread was changed by your leaving, and things began to seem unreal.

"Jesus," said the Moustache, "we've really done well today. Let's rest a while before starting up again. Getting the cards out is no big deal; we can have them done at Cisneros Printers and nobody'll be the wiser."

"Great," said Terezón, "it also gives us a good cover, a story better than anything we could have made up."

"At last," said Guayo, "between the orders for the spelling book and the business cards, things are definitely beginning to move; next we'll be hiring the night watchman to proofread for us."

That night I was too proud to go to the party. Later I found out that you danced all night, like the Princess of Monaco, with Roque. How ironic. And I spent the whole time lamenting the fact that I'd missed my chance, till I'd finally exhausted lamentation itself. You and Roque. A strange connection. A communicating vessel. Chance.

Then came your absence, your withdrawal, those things that were never clear: the murmur of life, the threads of that great mystery woven by time in the hands of Ariadne, or should I say the spider. And you, little bolero doll of long ago, once again you entered the place that everyone eventually enters, that cleverly made tunnel filled with a thousand traps. Or they made you enter. How did it happen?

"Right," said the Moustache, "I feel like new. Whaddya say we take the old bolt-bucket out for a spin now that it's not acting up?"

"Terrific," said Terezón, "but first don't forget to make the deal for the cards with Cisneros."

"Don't worry about it," replied the Moustache, pulling up the lever on the Multilith.

When everything was finally ready, Gonzalo appeared.

"Let's get this edition out tonight," he said. "They'll need it for tomorrow. The rumour is there's a coup coming. Everything should be ready and in the truck so we can move quickly. Meanwhile, why don't we go over to the Mundial to shake off the gloom." And that's where we ended up.

"Christ, there's nothing like a cold beer with a bowl of iguana soup," said the Moustache, licking his lips.

"Till nightfall anyway," said Gonzalo, letting out a thunderous burst of laughter that shook the Mundial from one wall to the other.

"Yeah, especially if you're alone," Terezón added ironically.

"Listen, we'd better go," said Guayo. "We don't want any fuck-ups."

"You're right," said Moustache. "Things could get sticky."

"Okay—since it's already eight o'clock, let's get the message out," said Gonzalo.

"Agreed," said Terezón, getting up from the table.

Another day. Another day in the life. In full sunlight. The way things go. You were alone. Just you. Neither Guayo nor the Moustache was there. This time there was just you,

Terezón.

The whole mess began that afternoon, Terezón, when you got the packages mixed up and sauntered over like someone on his way to a date who had hours to spare. It was Sofía herself who opened the door and put out her hands, into which you deposited the package, and after she signed you walked back slowly, probably thinking about the latest events to darken the country's skies.

As soon as you'd left, Sofía innocently opened the package. A dry wind struck her face; she was stunned; her eyes widened as she looked with growing surprise at those broadsheets calling for insurrection. Without a moment's hesitation, her emotions still running strong, she telephoned her husband and gave him a detailed account of the whole "unbelievable situation" and "outrageous event". He advised her to keep calm: he was just getting ready to leave for home.

Pale as a death mask, Sofía saw her husband assume the demeanour of a man who has discovered the key to a difficult problem after going through a pile of documents line by line; once he had put all the "reliable evidence" aside, he left the rest to time, and settled back with exaggerated impatience to wait through the long, scheming night, marking time till the break of day.

That's how it happened, at least according to the Chinese woman in Izalco's. That's how they burst in and began to beat you in their rage, kicking you as they dragged you out of Atlantis, without our knowing to this moment (or with our knowing and not wanting to accept) where you are, where your endless existence is flowering, just as no one will ever know "for sure" where this story begins or ends, a story as narrow and twisting as the corridor of the imagination down which the shadow of Sofía's image slowly disappears.

The Last Game

I know I'm dying: during the last few minutes—or hours?
—I've begun to feel detached from my body. I can hardly
make out the edge of the ravine I threw myself over trying
to escape. I wonder what's happened to Shorty and Blondie
and our friend Lenin? The game was great: skins and shirts.
I'd sunk three shots in a row and was just starting to get hot.
I only came to play to shake off my sluggishness and keep
in shape; these days you have to be in the best possible
physical condition to keep up with all the intense activity
going on. Those little bastards from Zacamil; if they'd
lasted to the end of the game, we would have tied it up.
There's no doubt about it: I didn't play well, but I couldn't
concentrate. How was I supposed to? Knowing that
afterwards you've got to go off to the— And that you can
die there.

I can hear distant voices and the murmur of the river. I
don't feel any pain except for a tingling in my stomach and
one hell of a thirst, and this humming like a swarm of
hornets in my left ear. The worst is that if I die I'll never see
our victory, and poor Aminta will scream like a madwoman
when she finds out I'm gone. What'll she do with the kids?
If this is dying, it's like casting off the great rock of the body
and falling into an enormous emptiness, as if the body were
a flat tire with the air leaking ou—

I can hear them calling me now . . . far away. I'm marching in the demonstration and we're shouting Freedom or Death, Freedom-or-Death, FreedomorDeath, and I'm carrying a huge sign and my friends Recinos and Stubby have their arms around each other's shoulders shouting *vivas* to the Popular Front. I don't feel my body at all any more, just a constant wet dripping on my chest. Now I hear the dogs of the city, off in the distance, barking as if sending news of my death to who knows whom, probably to other do—

(Come on, Pomponio, move it; the net's all yours. The ball falls right into my hands, round and clean; I take it and thr— It sails through the air in a perfect curve and swishes into the net. Hey, Manuel, Cirilo calls to me, take the flyers and come back as soon as you can, 'cause later you're gonna have to— Hello? Yeah, Rosario, you're speaking to him; yes, it's me, Manuel. What? You think what I'm doing is crazy? Sure, crazy like Martí. No, Rosarito, it's the absolute truth. Yes, yes, I found out: they grabbed them in Acajutla but they've already let 'em go because the rank and file said otherwise they'd go out on strike. Whaddaya mean, no? Listen, Rosarito, I'm telling you it's true. They're on their way right now. No, no, I won't forget; I'll tell you when he gets here. Sure. Take care, sweetheart.)

I'm playing once again. Sticky sweat; legs relaxed, flexible, agile; I can jump freely. Then I see the Cherokee with the tinted windows. It stops right on the corner; all four doors open and four guys with machine guns get out, while a fifth waits at the wheel with the motor running. At that moment the ball comes at me again like a black sun, hurtling through the air towards my hands. I make a pass to Pomponio; he passes to the Giraffe, the Giraffe to the Turtle and it's back in my hands ag— The men from the

Cherokee point me out, walk towards us aiming their guns. Pomponio, who's in front of me, is surprised when I refuse the ball, and even more when he sees the grimace of astonishment and fear in my face. The four men keep on coming and I run, terrified, swearing that if I had a gun I'd. . . . And I throw myself over the side of the ravine followed by bursts of fire and I fall into this hole and I see the fat guy aiming the barrel of his gun at my head to give me the *coup de gr . . . âce. . . .*

A Trivial Story

Victoria Ocampos was sobbing disconsolately, her bour-
geois tears stained with mascara and redolent of Max
Factor; her arms, resting elegantly on the steering wheel of
her Peugeot 304, were covered by the mass of her prema-
turely grey hair, which spread out like a shower of water
across half her face. Nobody came by this miserable
neighbourhood at that time of day; nobody, that is, except
Arturo Rimbó, who was just then returning from his first
day at work and was searching for a particular clandestine
restaurant, a little hut of sheet metal that gave off a sticky
smell of rib steak and onions. He was just going in when he
suddenly saw that the woman in the car parked in front was
crying. He had a timely, emotional hunch that something
serious was the matter, so he came closer and gave two
meticulous and solemn taps on the window and the woman,
Victoria Ocampos, raised her head, her face like a Chinese
mask.

"Can I help you in any way?" asked Arturo, looking
compassionately at her reddened eyes and her nose smudged
with mascara.

"It's all right, thanks," said Victoria Ocampos,
feigning a rictus of a smile, as if for Kolinos toothpaste.

"Then why the tears?" asked Arturo, starting to lay
a few plans.

"Well," answered Victoria, "the fact is, I'm going

through an enormous emotional crisis, and I couldn't really explain why, because there're so many reasons that—"

"There's no need to," Arturo volunteered, remembering a few pages from *Lessons in Urban and Civic Ethics.* "Let me buy you a coffee; maybe it will calm your nerves. The Black and White is just around the corner."

"Thanks," said Victoria Ocampos. "That would be wonderful. You're very kind."

"The fact is," said Arturo, "your face seems familiar to me."

"Maybe you've seen me in the newspapers," Victoria Ocampos affirmed. "I'm a well-known pianist and I work in TV."

"Ah, yes," said Arturo, feeling now that he was reaching the very summits. "On the program 'Search for the Stars', isn't it?"

"That's it," replied Victoria Ocampos, flattered. "But, I'm sorry, you're frying out there in the sun and I still haven't invited you in."

"Thanks," said Arturo, getting into a Peugeot 304 for the first time in his life and breathing in the smell of Victoria Ocampos's car. "That invitation to coffee still stands," he added nervously, overcome by it all.

"Fine," said Victoria Ocampos, closing the door of the Peugeot.

"Then why don't we go to the Chantilly," Arturo proposed, breathing in again and looking out the car window at the wretched huts.

"Whatever you'd like," said Victoria Ocampos, checking in the rearview mirror and wiping her nose with a tissue, "but first let me ask your name."

"Arturo Rimbó," said Arturo, settling back in his seat as if into a cloud as the car sped off, floating over the grimy street.

"But aren't you the poet who won that poetry competition in Quezaltenango and was interviewed in *Mundo*?"

"One and the same," Arturo averred, in a tone both falsely and truly humble.

"Well, what a coincidence!" said Victoria Ocampos. "Two nights ago I bought your book at a stand at the National Book Fair, and the moment I started reading it— and I'm not just saying this because you're here with me— I told myself, 'I've just got to meet this man.' Because, you know, the 'Friends of Art' meet at my home."

"Really!" said Arturo, feigning surprise and putting on his poet's face. "The book itself is nothing, but it might possibly be the beginning of something new."

"I feel you're actually more of a philosopher than a poet," continued Victoria Ocampos, turning on the radio.

"Not necessarily," replied Arturo, wriggling nervously in his seat. "It's only the influence of—"

"Excuse me," she interrupted, turning up the volume, "but this is my favourite song, 'American Woman', by the Guess Who."

"Oh yes, of course," said Arturo, looking at her even more intently and feeling like Julio Cortázar with the Sorceress, without understanding either the music or the English lyrics.

"Ah," said Victoria Ocampos, assuming an air of superiority, "music is such an experience, a great voyage. At home I've got the Grateful Dead and Jefferson Airplane and lots of underground magazines. Someday, if you want, I could lend them to you."

"That would be great," said Arturo, feeling as though he were travelling through clouds of hidden knowledge and arriving on another planet. "For me, music is like aspirin," he added.

"That's marvellous," the Sorceress affirmed, turning left onto Los Próceres Boulevard, half a block from the Chantilly. "My passion is music. I studied in Germany under Stockhausen, but I retired from playing when my husband was killed in an accident with a glider as he was driving home one night from Berlin."

"What a shame!" said Arturo. "Both for music and for your husband. I would so like to hear you play."

"Maybe someday," said Madame Rubinstein.

"And what would you like to drink with me today?" asked Arturo, in his poet's voice.

"Well," said Victoria decisively as she parked the Peugeot under the eaves of the Chantilly, "a pilsner."

"All right then," Arturo replied, learning to act like a man without complexes, "let's go inside and find ourselves a quiet spot."

The waitress came over immediately to Table 23.

"What will you have?" she asked, with a half-serious, half-amused expression.

"Two pilsners," replied Arturo, "please."

"What do you do besides write?" Victoria Ocampos asked him the classic cliché.

"I'm a proofreader," said Arturo, assuming the demeanour of a broker on the London Stock Exchange.

"How interesting!" Victoria Ocampos replied artfully, unfamiliar with the nature of such a Kafkaesque line of work. "It's a shame," she continued, taking a sip from her foaming beer, "that you had to meet me in such a deplorable state, but I've been going through a terrible time in my life. Maybe it's the memory of Karl."

"Could be," said Rimbó, taking the beer that Victoria offered him and knitting his brows paternally. "Solitude is like death for the living," he added sagely.

"But let's not talk of sad things," said Madame

Bovary, "especially today, when we've only just met."

"Don't worry about me," replied Arturo Pessoa with distress, as he looked at her admiringly, loving her at first sight and finding her gazing back at him with the same expression. The way she was holding her glass reminded him of Joan Crawford in "Sudden Fear".

"I hope we can see each other again," whispered Victoria Ocampos, seductively finishing her beer. "What time do you go back to work?"

"At three," Arturo answered, glancing surreptitiously at Victoria's bare calves and suddenly, with a mixture of resentment, love and guilt, remembering his wife and two sons sunk in their one-room apartment in the Honduras Rooming House.

"Well then," said Magdalena Bach, "I don't want to take up any more of your time."

"I'm happy to offer it," answered Arturo Dostoevski, thinking about how he would arrive late at the Diario Latino and of the pile of galleys that awaited him. "Do you have anything urgent today?" he asked hollowly.

"No," responded Joan Crawford. "My biggest problem is that I never have anything to do."

"All right then," said Rimbó, "let's have another beer, and you can tell me about yourself."

"The truth is," replied Wonder Woman, "there's so much I want to tell you that we'd definitely need more time to go into it all. And since I suppose we'll be seeing each other again soon, there'll be plenty of time to deepen our friendship. Maybe one night you could come over to my house in San Benito, and then. . . ."

"I'd be delighted to," said Super Mouse, full of curiosity and gallantry, like a man of the world who has a situation fully in hand. "Call me at the Diario Latino whenever you like and we'll—"

"Oh! What a shame!" the Sorceress moaned, looking at her watch. "It's three o'clock on the dot. I'll drive you back to work if you like."

"Okay," said Arturo (thinking, "I hope those bastards at the office see me with her and die of jealousy"). "That would be wonderful."

"After all you've done for me . . . " said Victoria Crawford, arranging her false eyelashes.

"In that case," said Rudolph Valentino, "I guess we'd better go."

"As you wish," replied Greta Garbo.

"It's been an unforgettable afternoon," said Arturo de Córdoba, taking out the only ten-colón bill in his wallet and giving it, with the air of a millionaire, to the girl, who was waiting attentively for a tip.

"You've been my guardian angel," remarked Lois Lane with a coquettish smile, as they listened to Creedence Clearwater in the car.

"Or is it just the opposite?" thought Arturo, reassuming his actor's pose and feeling himself float through the air as *la Ocampos* accelerated down the highway.

The Nahual

There were also nahuals, *or guardian spirits, who were kind: songbirds who knew how to shed tears when a beautiful girl died, birds whom the Moon surprised as they watered flowers on the tombs of their dead mistresses.*

I know a legend. It was during the reign of the tyrant Pilguanzimit that the lords of Ixtepetl raised the banner of rebellion. A bloody struggle ensued. The winter rains filled the craniums of thousands of skulls left staring at the sky. Cities, forests, everything was destroyed in the conflagration, and Death made its lair in our forests.

In the end many brave chiefs fell, and only far away, in the recesses of the mountains, did a single wild group of rebels find refuge. One of them was Apantl, daughter of a dead chieftain. She had her father's warrior spirit, and she and her followers launched repeated attacks against the tyrant.

Her nahual *was a black and yellow* chiltota *bird that rode into battle singing on her shoulder.*

One night Apantl wandered off from camp. The empire was at war. And her warriors never saw her alive again. In the morning they found her stiff, cold body with an arrow through her heart.

No longer was her warrior's cry heard in the fray; never again did her brave arm wave a battle-axe against the tyrant.

But in the flowering branches of the aromo *tree under*

—45—

which she had died, a chiltota *built her nest. The bird shook
the branches and covered the ground with flowers.*

     They say that one night the chiltota *also died. The
Moon saw her fall in the middle of her song, rigid and mute,
onto the carpet of flowers that she had spread herself.*

     There are no more kindly nahuals. *Or* chiltotas *on
flowering branches, who sing and cover tombs with flowers.
Oh beloved* nahuals, *who perished along with the race!*

     Miguel Angel Espino, "Los pájaros nahuals"

Well then. That day, like every other day, Salvador was
ironing a pair of pants, except that they weren't ordinary
pants because they belonged to Don Antonio Salazar, who
was at that time—because he's dead now—almost seven
feet tall; so the ironing-board was long and flat. Up there
in Salvador's house-study-workshop, there wasn't a single
one of God's afternoons during which his old friends would
fail to drop by. These included a little hunchbacked bolero
singer nicknamed Scales because he walked to one side, a
self-taught painter named Urraco Mendive, and a rural
schoolteacher and expert organizer whom everyone called
Pestalozzi. They used to meet together and talk and get
themselves all riled up, and over the years they had con-
verted Salvador's tailor shop into a royal academy of con-
spirators against the soporific boredom and machinations
of time.

     Salvador was at heart a reclusive man. Spools of
thread, sewing machines and silver thimbles shared the
solitude of his shop with a little bird that sometimes seemed
like a mandarin orange with wings, especially when it
fluttered above his head or hopped around his body, doing
a peripatetic balancing act on the pages of the newspaper he
read in the morning.

Thus, thanks to the extravagant imaginations of its visitors, the world of the tailor's shop was transformed into another space, where the world's realities converged in miniature and took on the markings and colouring of the nervous little bird. It goes without saying that it was also an extremely romantic milieu, in which the voices of Carlos Gardel, Antonio Méndez and Pedro Infante were often heard on the record player, and there were readings of the poetry of Neruda, Orlando Fresedo, Velarde and many others. At times there were discussions of avant-garde painting, and phrases were exchanged that made the painter Urraco Mendive's easel positively reel.

Salvador was a learned and mysterious man who concealed his poetry and drawings in the dusty disorder of his shop. He was also as powerful as a stallion—according to the hunchback Balanza—especially when it came to seducing young girls, which was why his life was filled with women and children (as *The Cid* would say). His incessant womanizing gave rise to rumours of pacts with certain spirits. Nevertheless, and this was the enigma of it all, he lived alone, his sole companion being the tiny bird, a kind of *nahual,* a symbol of his personal history, herald of his craft and of his untutored ingenuity of imagination. In addition to his other friends, Father Luis Manrique would also come by from time to time to drop off a bit of work or talk about the path to liberation. Estrella Domínguez—who is now famous in Madrid, where, according to Balanza, she's known as the "Queen of Boleros"—would stop in as well. People showed up from every corner of the city, some on utilitarian errands, others to kill time in the boring war of temporal attrition, though times were already beginning to show signs of changing. They all came to visit.

There are many tales of Salvador's wondrous acts, marvels and miracles, from his dexterity with sewing needles to his reputation as a calligrapher of renown, a poet and autodidact, an inventor of words and a daring photographer. It is said that his camera was the first to record the arrival of morning at the exact moment when night slinks around the corner just before dawn. But what is most often told is the incredible yet veracious story of his enchanted bird.

That bird, according to Doña Encarnación (Salvador's godmother), was no ordinary warbler: "You should've seen the little thing. Salvador used to throw it up into the air in that amazing way of his, so it would disappear into the sky and then come diligently back to nest on Salvador's head. There it would delicately alight, its master's very own exquisite little bird. But on March 19, at about four o'clock in the afternoon—the hour when Salvador always used to step outside for a breath of fresh air—the strangest thing happened: he lifted the bird down from his head and, in full view and hearing of everyone, jokingly suggested that it take off into the sky forever. Then he threw it up into the air, but this time, once it was aloft, the bird flew higher and higher up through every level of the sky, till it disappeared into the invisibility of the infinite. And yes, that's right: it never came back."

Salvador gave a wild laugh and returned to his shop, where he continued to cut, scissors in hand, along the line he had traced across a bolt of denim cloth, while the strangest thoughts went through his mind.

Then, according to Urraco Mendive, came a whole hell of those disasters that always ensue when you call the Devil to account. The little bird certainly never came back, not on your life, nor did Salvador ever recover his light transparency of being. But time didn't stand still just because of that; on the contrary, it kept on growing, putting forth new branches, disarming shadows, plotting. From the moment the bird flew off and failed to return, the hours, those approaching footsteps of old age, were transformed into centuries.

Everybody knows what happened afterward. Later that afternoon, as Salvador was ironing and listening closely, trying to follow the thread of what was being discussed in the get-together, a whole legion of hooded men armed with cattle prods and automatic weapons burst into the shop. Everyone there was tied up (on suspicion of being a terrorist), punched, kicked and dragged at gunpoint into a truck that took off noisily down the narrow road, and disappeared into the shadowed destiny forming in the eye of the tiny embalmed bird on Doña Encarnación's mantelpiece, the bird whose pupil reflects the hope of the world.

Know What I'm Sayin'?

One more beer—we were already plastered and totally stoned out on a fantastic vibe—know what I'm sayin'? So finally I split for home, but my folks were out, so I went by my old lady's place and there wasn't a fuckin' sound; she'd taken off to look for me at the demo that was set for three-thirty. What a bring-down, but I rebounded back to the Bis a little after three, where I ran into Lito again. The two of us went over and had a few beers in that old store on the corner and then that dude Luis showed up, smashed out of his mind, know what I'm sayin'? So from there he brought us over to his place, where there was some great smoke and fantastic rapping going down, and all at once Lito got up from the bed he'd crashed out on and went over to the record player and put on the Cream and that left us even more blissed out than before.

That's what we were into when someone tapped in code on the balcony window, and it turned out to be none other than Meme and Richard, who had just eased their heads a little via a toke or two with their personal pusher. And then we got into a monster rap about the university and the fuckin' profs, know what I'm sayin'? And right in the middle of it—tock, tock—somebody was tapping on the window again, and guess who it was? No less than the Cat himself, with a bottle of wine from Salandra's, who'd come to give our high another smooth boost up into space. We had a super-fantastic rap. In those days the Animal always had his eye on us. It must've been past four by then but I wasn't in a position to notice and we'd finally had enough and that dude Luis put the Marmalade and Doors albums back in their covers and we went out into the street and since my old lady was nowhere to be found I tried to figure where she could be and bam! I remembered the demo at three-thirty, so I asked the guys to drop me off at my old lady's place and they all smiled like idiots and left me at the Number Three bus-stop and when I got on and paid the two bits I couldn't believe it! My old lady was in the back seat and for a moment I hesitated, thinkin' it was a goddamn hallucination. But it certainly was my old lady, with her red beret and her T-shirt with the huge scorpion on it and her big eyes and sweet mouth. . . . Mmmmmuuuaaaammm! The uppest of ups and then bam! came the hugs and kisses and guys in the street were pointing at us and yelling, "Trash!" and then the old rattletrap veered off just past Rosales Hospital because the cops had blocked Highway 25 and were all turned out with their tear gas and riot gear, so we got off near Cuzcatlán Park and doubled back up via Arce, and after a lot of fuckin' around finally ended up in the scrub about two blocks from the Bis and between one thing and another went past the alley where that big landowner's mansion is and then past Pete's and we saw the demo had already started because the thing was on its way downtown so we slipped in right there behind Fat Irma who signalled to us with her hand so we passed on the news that the cops were dug in around the Social Security Building and were getting the worst of it and since we saw nobody much cared we went on singing and shouting and when we got down to the Social Security we saw the Animal come zooming in on us in their brand-new armoured cars.

And instantly the crowd took off over the fences and down the alleys and across the bridge and everything was getting pretty fucking heavy and wild because the cops had it to the floor and their armoured cars ran over some girls and you could hear bursts of machine-gun fire and my old lady and I were just starting to run when one of those goddamn tanks knocked her flat and drove right over her, draaagggging her along the pavement at the same time that a blow from a rifle butt opened up my forehead, so between the bullets and the screams of the crowd running around and the smoke from the tear gas they grabbed me and it wasn't till a week later when my head began to function again that I found out they'd locked me up on suspicion of being a subversive. You know what I'm sayin'?

Juan Trimpot

The oily smell of onions boiling in a casserole rose up to the fourth floor of the Salandra building and came in through the window of the Federation of Trade Unions office where Juan awaited the arrival of one of the directors. He watched the clock as it marked exactly seven, then went over to the window and looked out at the rooftops and clouds, the foliage of the bushes and the people walking down to the beach, because on Saturdays everyone goes to the beach. The smell of frying became stronger and more persistent, entering his nose and going straight down to his empty, hungry stomach, as it did every morning when he was ready for beans and cream, fried bananas, French bread and black coffee.

The La Caverna restaurant was located in a house as old as the Salandra building, which made its skeletal wattle framework stand out even more. Its only furnishings were five or six little tables with brightly coloured table-cloths near the doorway, and four other tables set closer to the kitchen, which was separated from the restaurant by a strip of cyclone fence. Juan always had breakfast at one of the tables in the back. Today, as he left the Salandra building, he looked around carefully, tucked his satchel under his arm and walked towards La Caverna, rediscovering the same scene that greeted him every morning: two prostitutes, Moby Dick and Tarzana, were leaning on the bar in the corner tavern; farther on, beyond the open sewer, stood the newspaper vendor and the shoeshine boy; and in the distance, near the Alcoholics Anonymous office, the same couple of drunks as always.

This morning, on entering the restaurant, he was surprised to find Carmen watching him from the table in the far corner. He walked towards her, making his way around the other customers, moved a bench over to her table and sat down across from her.

"Do you know where Federico left the newssheets?" he asked her, signalling to the girl in the kitchen to serve him his usual breakfast.

"Yes," Carmen answered, "but we'll have to wait till Mario comes: he's the only one with a key to the storage room."

"I hope he shows up soon," Juan replied, "because I've got to deliver them to the guys in the maquiladora district and then check on the petitions with the committee."

"He shouldn't be long," said Carmen persuasively, raising her coffee cup to her lips.

A half-hour later, three new clients entered La Caverna: Beto, a musician in the symphony orchestra; Lisandro, the watchmaker; and Manuel, the linotype setter from Cisneros Printing. Meanwhile Juan cleaned his teeth with his tongue as images of the duty-free zone rose up in his mind: machinery, smokestacks, thousands of hands, piles of garbage, ads—

"Damn! Time goes by too quickly. It's eight already," Carmen said. "But Mario will soon be here: I know he will. We agreed to meet at a quarter to."

"Let's give him ten more minutes on account of the buses," said Juan.

"Okay," answered Carmen, as her eyes surveyed

each of the customers.

At that precise moment, three armed men got out of a grimy Land Rover outside the restaurant. One of them came through the door and lowered the muzzle of his machine gun, while the other two stayed outside guarding the entrance until the operation was over.

The man next to the door opened fire directly into the crowd of people eating. China plates and cups shattered, making a metallic noise that Juan remembered from films about Al Capone. When the murderous firing stopped, a thick cloud of gunpowder and oil hung in the air. The three men got back in the Land Rover and drove coldly off.

The survivors gradually drifted over to the restaurant door, where they huddled together while the kitchen staff crawled out from underneath the counter. As the smoke cleared through the windows, the results of the attack became clear: blood-soaked corpses collapsed over plates of half-eaten food. And among them lay Juan, fallen over his satchel.

Carmen's life had been miraculously spared, though she'd been wounded in the leg and had to be taken to hospital in a taxi.

Reporters began to arrive. Juan had been killed. Juan Trimpot. Mario walked into the union office and told them, "They've just killed Juan." Other union members arrived from the maquiladora district and were told, "Juan's been killed." And the news spread by word of mouth to every part of the city.

"Can you tell me," the France-Presse correspondent asked Mario, "the full name of the murdered trade unionist?"

"No," answered Mario, "we only knew him as Juan. Juan Trimpot, because he represented the union members of Trimpot Incorporated."

¿Qué Hi?

... and there I was, my friends, walking in a night full of diamonds with my buddy Suncín, both of us drunk as farts, staggering through the Escalón one Sunday, dropping our money in nightclubs and our hands into drunks' pockets, a great fantastic life eating like kings and screwing rich old ladies, rapping and flying around on the latest wheels, living it up. Man, I almost felt like Marlon Brando himself in one of his best takes, and so between one bash and another it was finally midnight and the old ladies took off back to their old men and we ended up near the Safari and looked in to see what was happening and inside there were some rich bastards talking business and at another table some really old guys with their decked-out elegant old ladies and we started to set something up because, you know, right there in the dark in the middle of the show starring Zaza Gabor and the Salvadoran Brigitte with spicy salsa music, the Animal was watching, and you can never tell who they're going to come down on next, so we kept checking things out till we saw some other suspicious-looking characters drinking endless beers and Suncín gave me the sign that they were cops and we split back out onto the street to get some fresh air just when the Aretha Franklin of Panama was winding up her show by smoking a Havana cigar with her cunt.

Outside everything was cool as usual with a nice

little breeze coming down from the volcano and we began to walk and walk, tripping out on the unbelievable wheels that seemed newer and shinier than anything I'd ever seen before, and we cased out an MG and opened the door with a wire without being spotted by the Animal or any night watchman, and bam! we got into the car and that new-car smell hit us superfine and even better when we slipped the passkey to her and she started up clean and I pushed down on that little virgin accelerator and we blasted out of there, man. And then as we were going down Beethoven I put on the radio just when Mama Cass's beautiful voice comes belting out with a tremendous wail and after that it was Hendrix with riffs like bursts of machine-gun fire spraying our ears, unbelievable and totally out-of-sight. That's what we were into when we heard the Animal's siren behind us but when were they ever going to catch us with a wonder car like that? So we danced them a mambo through the city and traffic, flat out down the boulevard all the way downtown, where we messed up their heads and lost them and then took off north down Trunk Road in that car that hauled ass like a mother and leapt over potholes like cotton clouds. We were just starting to think how sweet it was going to be showing off to all the chicks and brothers in the neighbourhood when the cops suddenly bounced out of the darkness onto the Trunk. I punched it to the floor and jammed it left and we took off down Atlacatl Road where we finally ended up smashing that beautiful machine into a wall.

When we opened the door we were met by a storm of punches, kicks and blows with billy-clubs; one cop put a gun barrel in my goddamn ass and got so worked up he was frothing at the mouth. They knocked Suncín to the ground with a pistol-butt and kept screaming "fuckinhippietroublemakers terrorist carthieves kidnapper robbersonsofbitches" and they lifted him up off the ground by the hair and tied us up so tight the rope broke and the second time we lost all feeling in our hands because they turned purple and went numb.

They took us to a basement where the Head Animal took charge of the third degree: so where was the minister, what faction did we belong to, who did we steal cars for? The whole thing turned out to be a huge fucking hassle because as the cop ranted on we found out that the same night somebody had dragged the minister or whoever the fat cat was out of his house and every cop in the city was hunting for the guys who'd done it, and since we didn't squeal the guy put wires on our balls and gave us the "Russian salad", hooking us up to electrodes that sent the current from our feet to our ears by way of our noses, and the first jolts made us bleed like crushed strawberries and at the same time another fucking cop kept hammering us with his truncheon.

And that, brothers, is how we woke up, and after beating on us some more they left us in a pile, gasping like fish in pools of our own blood. Then I went into a long black dream, and after that a heavenly song came out of the night and suddenly it was as if the sky were opening and Number One Himself and His archangels and the whole orchestra of bugles and electric guitars were announcing the end of the world, and then it was like in a movie or a mirror, I saw myself the night I stabbed the old lady who caught us robbing her grimy little store and we tied her to a chair and emptied all the beers in her refrigerator just for fun until the neighbours came to see what was going on and the old lady's kids showed up with guns and we split like lightning into the night jumping over backyard fences and then fell into the street on top of some guy who happened to be walking by—and they never picked up our scent because we took off a second later in the yellow Beetle. About a century or maybe a minute later I woke up to the screams of Suncín who was rolling around on the floor covered in blood and then I saw everything in blue and on the horizon there was a superfine park full of green and my old lady was sitting on the grass in a blouse with a picture of Che Guevara on it that kept goddamn moving and then the whole landscape suddenly began turning into a ball of thread that was being dragged along by the foot of a red bird that came zooming down into my navel and then I saw myself inside a car getting it on with that girlfriend I used to have in Room 16 and I heard her delicious moaning and the radio playing "Lucyenescaay / witdaimons" and you could see the waves of music coming through the air. But then everything went dark and goddamn depressing again and the sun appeared out of the darkness like a black disk and you could hear it fall into the waters of the sea that came roaring up in gigantic waves that splashed over the mountains and were so enormous they knocked down eighty-storey buildings and followed us with huge toothless mouths.

The cop had tossed a bucket of cold water in my face and I began to remember I was locked up and I saw Suncín shaking the water from his head and they'd worked him over so bad that his face looked like somebody else's. Then the cop punched us in the head to show us we had to stand up and after about a thousand years we finally managed to get up on our legs that were shaking like crazy and once we were standing everything began whirling around again and I puked for hours and hours and when I'd finished they dragged us back for interrogation.

And it began all over again, the whole spiel with him showing us the photo of the minister and offering to set us free and send us out of the country if only we gave him important information about our cell and the other terror-ists and when we couldn't answer he sent us back down to the basement and they put us through the Russian salad I-don't-know-how-ma-ny-times again with shocks to our balls every fifteen minutes and with the radio on full blast until that night they took us to some special kind of cop lab where a shrink shot us up with a drug that makes you tell the truth and a few minutes later I saw the heavens opening up again but this time full of blood because the whole earth was spattering them and then came German tanks and millions of soldiers with faces like Hitler and then a huge rotten green fish as big as a country while I heard a voice yelling questions at me again about the terrorist cell and the minister, the terrorist cell and the minister, the terrorist cell and the minister. In the middle of all this I saw a great thick cloud that my old man fell out of, he fell out and ran off down a blind alley of some city in the States like New York where my old man actually lives and then for some reason he came running back again. Everything was like a huge noisy movie because you could hear "Black Dog" in the background. And after about half a century I heard the cops screaming at us and I woke up in a cell where other guys were laughing at us like crazy and I couldn't handle it so I got up as well as I could and kicked the worst one of them in the face and then everything broke loose in a huge brawl and all the prisoners began to yell till a couple of cops came and opened the cell and dragged us out of there hitting and hitting us and threw us in another cell and from then on I never saw Suncín again, my friends, because they put me in the nuthouse and broke me down with electroshock every time I told them that I'm El Salvador and here I am brothers they've got my number and know I'm not lying or bullshitting when I tell them I'm El Salvador, the goddamn Saviour of the World.

The Better to See You

It was in her final hours that her seriousness, which had always been so typical of her, suddenly disappeared. "She's got such a strong character," Aunt Antonia used to say. But she became as gentle as a river seen from afar, a silver thread winding through valleys and lowlands. She ceased to be the woman who once, in a fit of anger, asked me to give her back a beautiful silver plate with engravings by some skilled craftsman of the Old World. What was it that caused her resentfulness that day? I don't remember now. But the incident happened. Perhaps it was simply her solitude, those long years of living alone, the helplessness she felt ever since the afternoon when grandfather slammed the door and went off, never to return.

My grandfather had once had thousands of head of stock, from oxen and Arabian stallions to purebred sorrels. His ranch, which is still called "Los Olivares", was far up the slopes of the volcano; he later lost it during a run of bad luck while playing dice. Everything went: the houses, the horses —his whole immense fortune.

Forty years had passed since then. Forty years in which my grandparents never saw each other again, during which my grandfather seduced scores of women and ac- quired a couple of decrepit houses—real shacks, according to Aunt Isabel. Forty years for death to finally overtake him.

That night when my grandmother started to become

delirious and say strange things, she travelled down a road without beginning or end. A road as green as the Sacred Valley. There, as she sought refuge in the shade of a flowering apple tree, just as she was getting ready to rest, her husband Moisés suddenly appeared, so white he was almost transparent. He came over to the apple tree and told her, "You shouldn't be travelling this road in those clothes. They won't be needed where you're going."

The next day, when the fever had subsided and she was lucid again, Grandmother opened her eyes and saw all her children and grandchildren standing around her, steeling ourselves to face her final departure. She told us about the thousands of naked women she'd seen on that vast grassy plain, some sprawled on the ground, others dancing old waltzes of days gone by. It had been a great delight to stretch out on that cushion of grass, infinitely more comfortable than her own bed, which was hard as rocks. She asked the women of the family to remove her dress.

So they did take off her clothes and bathe her in rose water—at her request—but when they wanted to spray her with Desert Flower perfume, she picked up the bottle and threw it outside against the rocks. Afterward they covered her with fresh blankets whiter than flour and brought her back to her bed. Then she cried out, "I forgive you, Moisés!"

Again she started down that road, the one that led to heaven, a long and sinuous path of flowers and thorns. God was waiting for her at the other end.

Almost awakening, she told her children that her feet hurt, for she had walked for years until she found eternal bliss; she said the pain was terrible. Whereupon Aunt Soledad took some Vick's VapoRub from her purse and rubbed her feet with it till they shone, while María, my foster sister, put a pill in her mouth.

Under the intense effects of the drug, she began to rise up into the clouds, blending into the ether of eternity. She made her way forward, pushing aside those great curtains of silvery morning mist, moving onward, tearing open the veils of that most unreal reality, subjected to the whirlwinds of heaven and hell.

She walked in paradise; she slept on the thick grass in the shadow of the apple tree. No taste, she later declared, could compare with that of those apples. It was useless to attempt to describe them, so she communicated their form, colour and taste by simply pressing her lips together and drawing them apart with a slight snap of expressive exquisiteness.

A few minutes later she asked us to bring her some apples, and in moments a crate of shining red California delicious was set before her. But a single bite was enough for her to reject their awful taste. Next she asked for a bowl of milk and we brought her some Nestlé's, and again she spat out chalky liquid that in no way compared to the river of milk and honey that meandered through the meadows of the Promised Land.

A few hours before dying, her breathing was transformed into a total exhalation, fragrant with the smell of moss, of her living daily breath. Her breathing was what was surest on that last winter morning.

Before she left us, Grandmother said that she would pass out the flowers. The ones she'd cut in paradise. Flowers of all scents and colours. There were blue ones for my cousin Teresa and yellow and green ones for my brother Miguel. For me there were white ones, the most invisibly real in all of paradise, which was open to everyone. Then, after handing the last flower to Aunt Soledad, my grandmother expired.

Uncle Gabriel, who some months later went off to

Brazil, told me that at that moment people sensed and heard an enormous bird flying through the sky. Don Torcuato López Tasso, an authority on the laws of gravity, used to say—because he too is now dead—that a tremor measuring six on the Mercalli Scale shook the earth that day and made the walls and beams creak. Antonio Yuko, a professional fly-catcher during Padre Piñota's masses, still tells how, at the very instant Grandmother died, he regained consciousness and complete rationality. Every household has more than one story about what happened that day; everyone knew about Grandmother's enchanted world and (sometimes endlessly) praised her strength and clarity of spirit.

And yet, of all the things that went on that day, I myself have always held on to the image of my parents pacing impatiently from one end of the room to the other, gesticulating, adding things up, worried about the cost of the burial, which was of course much more in those days of desperate poverty. I can still see and hear the moths and termites laying waste to that enormous three-part wooden wardrobe, on the other side of which my parents and aunts and uncles exhaled dense clouds of nervous and pensive smoke that day. I listened to the wearing away of that enormous wardrobe, the irritating little musical sound produced by its slow destruction, beneath my parents' whispers.

They spoke of this and that and wondered howtheheckmuch the tax on the gravesite would be. They discussed prices, appraised choices and finally decided that "a vault in a mausoleum would cost an arm and a leg," because "death has become a luxury" and "is a business loaded with traps." You could hear the reasoning behind their thoughts; you can still hear it in me today.

That night they finally found the key to the problem.

They buried her in the patio beneath the flowering guava tree. In the old wooden wardrobe. From which they removed the door, replacing it with a sheet of glass. Which stood up to the first shovelful of earth.

All that was a long time ago, but we still have a problem with people who are resentful and won't speak to us. They think we're strange and haughty because we didn't invite them to the funeral.

Sweet Home

I was about seven years old then and we were living in Number 56 of La Providencia Apartments. Tila, my mother, had a stall in the market, and every day at five in the morning we'd start dragging out our box of goods to sell and putting things in a cart that had a licence and was painted red and blue and was driven by Milo, Tila's younger brother, who was actually a lot closer to my age. There were over five hundred of us living in the tenement house, and it was nice because you could really have fun running around from one room to another spying on them all, learning lots of strange things and playing all sorts of tricks on people, because everybody saw and knew everything about everybody else. I remember that the Bebeleches lived there, the ones who were always so well decked out and never worked, though my older cousins used to say that they did work, but only at night, doing who knows what. Carlitos also lived there then. He was a silversmith who made rings and all kinds of sparkling jewellery that he used to give Tila sometimes when he'd come to see her at night and I'd pretend to be asleep. Then there was old Chiyate, who had a shoe repair shop, Fashion Elegance, in Number 5, where Beto Pliers, Mario Three-Balls, and Victor Shinola all used to work, and they'd give me scraps of leather so I could make shoes for my doll.

I can't remember much about the others because

there was a bunch of them, like Teri Grassmat, who never left her room because she was always locked up in there with all those guys who came to see her. Anyway, that's where we all lived in those days: my grandmother, Tila, Milo and me.

It was on one of those early mornings when we went with Milo to drop off the goods in the market that we heard the noise of a huge procession of people going into church for a wedding with bridesmaids and a flower girl and elegant ladies and their men all dressed up in the latest styles from Paris Volcano. The path to the church door was covered with pine branches and all you could see in any direction were cars and more cars, every one of them brand-new.

Once the bride and groom had entered and gone up to the main altar, Milo and I made our way through the crowd and up the stairway to the bell tower to look at the bells; that's how we found out it was filled with musicians playing the Wedding March as loud as they could up there, and as we stood watching them, the sacristan, Pedro Hurray-for-the-War, spotted us and dragged us out by the ears, calling us little brats. We didn't leave completely, though, but stood backed up against the wall to one side of the door so we could see how big shots got married. They were like people out of a movie: guys with rich men's faces looking at the priest without blinking as he came down and anointed the couple with holy oils to unite them for the rest of their lives, even though they might end up fighting (at that time I didn't know that even rich people fought after they got married), like Juana and David used to do every weekend at dinnertime.

After they were married, the fancy people all came out of the church in time to the music and the bells rang and a million startled doves flew out of the bell tower as people crowded together on the porch to wait for the splendid happy couple to emerge.

At that point all the ladies from the market, except for Tila, left their stalls and came to get a look at the splendid happy couple and all the guests, who were now getting into their cars and heading for the casino. Milo and I also took off down the cobbled street, running along joyfully, following the wedding party, and when we got to the casino we made our way inside in the midst of all the hubbub, and everything in the ballroom was incredibly bright and shimmering with balloons and streamers.

The orchestra played "María Cristina Always Tells Me What to Do", and all the guests were dancing gaily and light-heartedly. During one of the numbers Milo snuck into the kitchen and swiped a huge plate of food—things neither of us had ever tasted before—and we went outside to eat it on the sidewalk, savouring it like lords.

After that we went in again and got right up close to the Polío International orchestra and watched the maestros, who were redder than tomatoes, blow into their cornets. Then, still dying of hunger, we slipped through the crowd into the kitchen, where we spotted a giant keg full of soda and were drinking "grapettes" when a grouchy old lady came in and chased us out the door with an enormous stick. When we got outside, we found a crowd of people had gathered outside the windows to enjoy watching all those fine people enjoying themselves, and when we tried to get back in through a window that old pot-bellied guy they call The Raccoon started jabbing us in the ribs. So we decided we'd better go home—at least we'd eaten all we could—and since it was already past two in the afternoon I asked Milo to make a knot in his handkerchief for good luck so we wouldn't get thumped when we got there, but since neither of us had a handkerchief we made knots in our shirttails and went running home a bit scared.

When we got to the tenement house we went in softly—in slow motion—down the corridor. Grandmother was standing at the door, and to our surprise she didn't hit us like other times for being no-good troublemakers; instead she called us over very quietly and told us that Tila had been taken to the hospital: she'd drunk a bottle of poison that afternoon, despondent that my father had gotten married that day.

And Proudly Proclaim Ourselves Her Sons

> "Let us salute our motherland,
> And proudly proclaim ourselves her sons."
> *National anthem of El Salvador*

In the room there is a folding screen, behind the screen a bed, in the bed a woman. Under the bed a chamberpot. The woman is lying down; her legs are open like the doors of a sarcophagus. Where they join, there is a spider's web, like an obliging trap or a machine for transformations. Whoever enters this door leaves through the other side of night with a mark on his forehead, a mark that makes him different for the rest of his life. He has been possessed instead of possessing; a victim of curiosity, he has won his first death. After facing certain death in the woman's tentacles and climbing up onto her body and being trapped between her long thick legs, nothing is ever again the same.

He has finally arrived at the woman's centre, his member erect, blade unsheathed; from his forehead, streaked with curiosity, a few drops of frozen sweat are running down his nose. Behind him, waiting their turn, are Manuel, Mario, Baltazar, Chus, Adrián, Fat Freddy, the Puente brothers. As he moves on top of The Giantess, he thinks of his father and mother. The old man is probably smoking Casinos as he reads the evening paper; she's listening to the rosary on the radio. He also thinks of Elena and Teresa lying on the grass, of their bodies smelling of the first rains, of wet earth.

Like a beast that raises clouds of dust. His first "dust": he's struggling. The Giantess whispers in his ear, perhaps to calm him, that once, in another time, his grandfather, his father, his uncle, his father's brothers and their sons as well were all like him now. She smiles; at her age it seems a great honour to have made men out of some fifty generations of males, out of half the town, from Don Rufino Palacios, the mayor, who must be in his eighties by now, to Dr. O'Connor, the Torres brothers, the sons of Rosona (daughter of Don Guillermo Dueñas, owner of the pawnshop), who in turn was the grandson of Don Tomás, an aged economist who used to spread his money out on a grass mat to dry in the sun.

He keeps on struggling. Moving. The Procession of the Holy Burial passes by in the street; he hears their rattles; the glow of the torches of the Brotherhood of the Holy Burial almost reaches them. At that moment The Giantess's skin becomes softer and he feels her enormous breasts becoming inflamed, like warm balloons. He remembers the brilliant attribute of her womb: Ah, Merciful Womb! Forever fresh, forever sweet! The interminable *taca tataca* of cords holding up the bed makes him think they are about to break.

The Giantess, her eyes fixed on the ceiling, is almost indifferent, like an immense river of flesh, a gelatinous mass lying there on the bed, sweat trickling from every pore, because the damned heat is inescapable unless it rains, but no, it can't be: a bit of air is actually coming in through the window, and on the other side of the screen he hears the voice of Mario making some foul remark, followed by a burst of sarcastic laughter, then, afterwards, the Daughters of Mary chanting a eulogy, "Blessed is the fruit of thy womb, which is Jesus!", that's coming from somewhere out near the Columbus bridge.

His head has started to swirl. A candle on the floor by the bed seems like a light from hell; his heart is pounding in an accelerating *tumbo tutumbo* that reaches the left ear of The Giantess, who imperturbably asks him to finish up now once and for all; there are other clients to attend to. The light of the candle is about to go out and the natural sin of the flesh is igniting in his body; on the opposite wall he can half-read, "Vote for General J sé M ía L mus on the 19th." It's hot.

"Haven't ya finished yet, sonny?" shouts The Giantess impatiently, while their navels squish together in a sweaty *chas chas*, almost in time to the music on the jukebox. The Giantess's body smells of rancid cheese, cheap talcum powder, amulets, mint, lemons, but also of the skin of eternity; her hair smells like bark and eucalyptus leaves. Her face must once have been beautiful; her legs, in spite of the years, are as massive as two columns holding up a house, energetic, enormous, so long that they hang over the side of the bed. The music on the jukebox is growing strident. More dirty laughter from Mario out there, and then suddenly a hot shower of semen spurts out of the erect dove, as from a hose, and the ceiling of the hut spins convulsively with the shaking of the bed.

The others are banging hard on the blinds.

"Be patient, you bastards," The Giantess yells angrily, as their bellies gradually stop their contortions.

He jumps quickly from the bed and pulls up his pants; he feels like running through the streets. While he is buttoning up his fly, The Giantess squats down over the chamberpot, a towel in her hand. The water drips milkily from the jug of her belly, as from a mountain onto ferns, palely; setting off a melody of little bells, the water falls to the glistening white bottom of the basin like a shower of silver, *din don din chirlilin chin chin*. The Giantess raises herself back up onto the bed and adopts the same position, the one she had at the beginning, and waits for the next in line.

At that moment, as he rounds the edge of the screen, he meets Mario, who is coming in with long strides, smiling and lascivious. He is able to hear the newcomer mounting The Giantess, who begins again, as in some ancient ritual, and with her own pure pride, to celebrate the religious services of her body, using the same phrases as ever: "Your daddy was here, who was the son of Don Adrián, who also passed through and was himself the grandson of General Trabanino, who in turn fathered five sons with that girl Florcita Casamalhuapa, all of whom came here as well and two of whom became army officers and even presidents later on and then had sons with Lucita Fajardo and Margotía Duarte, sons who had their turns here too, as did their sons, and those of the ones who married Doña Concepción Guerreros, your mother, who had two other sons by General Martínez, both of whom came here and are your cousins on your mama's side, and now you're here and who knows, perhaps some day the sons of your sons and their sons as well."

My José

We arrived back yesterday, Doña Lionor, and you can't imagine how changed we found the place: stuff strewn all over the yard, overdue bills; they'd even cut off the phone. So we've had more than enough to do, but thanks to my José, we've managed to put everything in order. This morning we unpacked our things and what a happy surprise to find two little gourds full of sweets from Aguacayo. You're a perfect mother-in-law, Doña Lionor: you never said a word about them; you had it all figured out before-hand. You can't imagine how happy the Chamorros were to receive the decorations the prisoners make in the peni-tentiary. They told me they were going to send you a note to thank you for the souvenirs, so expect to get a letter from them sometime in the next few days. As for our daughter, she's already begun her classes, and even though she'd have loved to stay with you, I think it would be best if she spent a year or so more here with us, because as you know back home it's only the children of the rich who get a good education, and things are getting so expensive that parents don't really have time any more to give their children the attention they deserve, so I think we'd better hold off for the moment if it's all right with you.

The same goes for José. I pray God to keep him from ending up on the wrong road or getting involved with bad people, and I ask Him to keep José just as he is now, well-behaved and serious about his work in the hotel, where the owner, a man named Von-something, is certainly taking good care of him for me, because he's promised to give him the night shift so José can keep taking his English lessons in the morning because right nearby, just two blocks away, as they say here, there's a school that's supposed to be excellent—it's where all Don Jaime's children studied—and that's where José wants to enrol, because he needs to keep himself busy with something all the time so he's not always thinking about going back home again or running around all over the place with his good-for-nothing friends, since it was on account of those guys, who were always drunker than skunks, that he got fired from the bank in the first place. No, Doña Lionor, it's not the same here, and though it's true that you earn more, you work for it, but the effort's worth it, because if someday you go back home to live, you'll be able to have a place of your own to settle down in, especially if it's some respectable little house like the one the Lorenzanas have there, with a nice little garden full of resedas and lion's foot—above all a place for the kids, since in the end we're not really important, it's the kids who are. This is what I tell my José and if you could only see how much better he is now you'd be as happy as could be. Today as I'm writing you, at this very moment, he's sitting here in the living room, and since he loves politics he's reading one of those books they send him from the bookstore on Richlan Street, where he's taken out a subscription for the rest of the year. The only thing I warn him about, Doña Lionor, is to be careful with politics because we're in a different country now and you've always got to obey the law. What's more, you should see how the Immigration police are always after people here; just a little while ago they grabbed two young guys as they were coming out of the Azteca Café where I work. I've been taking night shifts there, filling in for a friend of mine who's just had a baby. The money's going towards buying a car for my José, because a certain Mr. Rodríguez, who I suppose you must know since he says he lived in the Regalados' rooming house and had a little mechanic's shop where he used to do repair work, came over last month and said he could get us one. So we've agreed that we'll put all our cash together and look for a bargain on one of those little cars like the one Ronal has, remember? Because nowadays gas is so expensive that it's not worth getting one of those big ones. My José is really excited about the idea. I understand because I know he still remembers the shops along the street at home, and Tan Yada's store in particular, since they grew up together. It was only the other night that he was killing himself laughing, remembering Tan Yada's pranks when they were in school. I got a kick out of his stories because he said that in those days Tan used to sneak chewing tobacco from his father Don Habrán's personal tobacco pouch, and that he spent his time in class endlessly chawing on it, and because of that, he said, Don Juan Ventarrón, the schoolteacher, would punish him, but the kid was already hooked, maybe from watching his dad because as far as I can remember I never saw Don Habrán without a plug of tobacco in his mouth. That's why his teeth are all yellow, but the funny thing is that when he was older he broke the habit and when we were back this time we saw how he's straightened out his life and his store is really looking up. My José, who sends you all his best, also told me about the birds of good luck. I laughed when he described the thrashing you gave him when the bird vendor who turned out to be none other than Sixto Bividor complained that your son had stuffed all those birds in a bag, grabbing the chance when Sixto lay down to take a nap on the sidewalk steps. The poor old guy: I remember him because he always went around in huaraches and a cotton poncho for a blanket, and what's more, he was good at curing illnesses and driving evil spirits away from children, but you should have seen the way it made me laugh to hear my José tell that story. Nevertheless, I've been pretty depressed because of something I really regret, which is that maybe it was a little selfish of me not to stay that night in Margotilla's house, since she'd come by specifically to invite me over because she'd made a whole batch of tamales with *chipile*, and I still regret not going because she must have thought I looked down on her, but if you remember, that day I had a splitting headache that just wouldn't let up, maybe deep down because I was so worried about my José who hadn't been seen or heard from for several days, because as you know when he gets drunk he goes crazy and starts thinking about suicide, like the last time when he heard the national anthem and then threw himself out the apartment window and lay there half dead in the neighbours' backyard. Luckily we live on the second floor—if not. . . . So tell Margotilla to forgive me and I'll take a raincheck.

As I wrote you in my last letter the Immigration police are getting worse all the time; there isn't a blessed day they don't go from one building to another, one factory to another, one hotel to another, looking for illegals. Lately they've even started going into movie theatres and schools. As for us, we don't have too much to worry about because there aren't many Latinos where we work and that's an advantage because they don't suspect us. Oh, it's such a shame to see so many people keep coming into this country, some of whom arrive so full of hope and the country just isn't what it used to be. If you've got a steady job you've got to hang onto it because things are getting worse all the time. That's what I tell my José. God willing, as I told you, we'll save up a little nest egg and then see what we can do, because things in this country are not like they used to be when we first got here. Please write my José and tell him to be patient and not to drink, because we've got to make this time while the kids are little really count, when they start growing up things will be a lot harder.

I want to tell you too, though it's very painful, that I've had to put young Jorge into a special school because he was starting to turn out wrong. Imagine, first we found some of those little papers in his bookbag, like the ones Aunt Luz used to roll her homemade cigarettes with, and next I started to notice that he was always going around with his eyes as red as a demon's, though up till then nothing went beyond a few suspicions; but one night, I'm telling you, his room was filled with more smoke than a burning kitchen. He was turning into a little drug addict, Doña Lionor, and that's one thing I won't stand for. Did we come up here just so he could get corrupted and pick up bad habits? No, that's where I draw the line, Doña Lionor. All this has had a big effect on my José, but little by little he's started to understand how I feel, that it's always best to cut a vice like that off at the roots.

As for everything else Doña Lionor it's all going well. Even the weather has changed and it's sunny now. I think the winter is over and spring has come. What I can't stand is the cold, especially when it's windy, that icy wind that sweeps down the street here. But I think the worst has almost ended and soon, as we've planned with my José, we'll start going on picnics because there are some magnificent beaches near here. Though not like our beaches, that's for sure; I wouldn't trade our beaches at home for anything in the world. Here you can't really swim because the water's cold even in summer, but it is beautiful to walk on the beach and be out in the sun, and sit in the sand and look off in the distance and see the ships sailing out to sea and then you suddenly shut your eyes and start thinking about your own homeland out there, about sitting under the nanche and mango trees, smelling the *quequeishques* after one of those God-Almighty storms, and walking through the neighbourhood streets, those narrow little cobbled ones, and you can even smell the nice hot ears of corn cooking at suppertime. Everything comes back to me, Doña Lionor, even the songs of the parrots. That's why I understand my José, who gets very upset about all this, but nonetheless I remind him that it's always been like this and that he has only to think back on the Vidrís, the Llorts, the Millets, and how they arrived from faraway lands as naked as jaybirds.

I encourage my José—don't think I don't, Doña Lionor—and incidentally he's becoming more and more like his grandfather, as you yourself have said, in both physical strength and intelligence—because you should see how people from our country and from other countries too are always coming by to talk with him about what's happening in the world today, about famous governments and politics. Especially about our country and what a horrible mess it's in.

Whenever I hear about all those awful things, Doña Lionor, I don't want to go back. What would we be returning to? Here at least there's enough work to get by on and my José's little girl, who by the way I love as if she were my own, and my two sons all have their future assured.

Well, Doña Lionor, I guess I've said enough. Take care of yourself and make sure you take your medicine on time and stop worrying about your José, because I take care of my José as if he were my very own.

Adelia

Short Fiction from El Salvador

Two circus performers, a clown named Rafael Antonio Cartagena, sixteen years old, and a dancer named Sandra Patricia Beltrán, aged fourteen, both of whom work for the Blanquita circus, were kidnapped by terrorists on the night of January 5 and taken to a clandestine camp. They later managed to escape from their captors and are now under the protection of the armed forces of the Arce Battalion, which is currently carrying out search-and-destroy missions against terrorists in the departments of Usulután and San Miguel.

According to informed sources, the young clown, who is a native of the port city of La Libertad, and the dancer, who is from the national capital, were spending the evening of January 5 in Jucuapa, Department of Usulután, where they were participating in a circus performance, when the city was unexpectedly invaded by a large number of armed extremists who began to harass the artists and spectators, both young and old. The two youngsters, who have succeeded in escaping from their kidnapper's encampment, say that the terrorist assault was so sudden and rapid that the authorities who were guarding the town did not have time to repulse it. The terrorists quickly fled back into the mountains, taking various young people and adults of both sexes with them, among them the clown's uncle, José Eugenio Cartagena, nicknamed "Microbe". The elder

Cartagena, along with many other victims, is still in the hands of the terrorists, who are holding them under tight guard; according to the two young kidnappees, the victims are poorly fed and are under threat of death if they try to escape.

Both the young clown and the dancer have told military authorities in the Arce Battalion that after being beaten and abducted along with many other victims, they were interned in a terrorist camp in the canton of Las Marías, Department of Usulután, where they were left tied up for several days. The young clown and dancer were subsequently released from their bonds and told that henceforth their pseudonyms were to be "Joel" and "Janet", respectively, and that for the time being their mission would be to distribute subversive propaganda along the neighbouring roads and highways, as well as on nearby farms, but that every time they were sent on one of these missions, they would be kept under surveillance by two or three heavily armed terrorists who followed at a distance. The two youngsters affirmed that when they carried out their assignments, their guards would hide in the undergrowth and aim their rifles at them so they could not escape.

They added that they were kept for more than a fortnight in the guerrilla encampment in Las Marías Canton and then transferred to a site in the rural jurisdiction of Jucuarán, where the subversives maintain another camp. They were finally able to escape from the latter locale in the rural jurisdiction of Jucuarán by availing themselves of a moment's inattention on the part of their guards in order to run off into the forest, which they traversed during the night, arriving at the highway at dawn. When detained by military personnel of the Arce Battalion, they put their hands over their heads and asked to be protected. The aforesaid personnel from the Arce Battalion were carrying out a terrorist reconnaissance patrol in the adjacent territory when they discovered the two fugitives. Both were placed under immediate protection and taken to battalion headquarters, where they told all that has been heretofore described, without any threat of pressure or force.

The two kidnappees reported that the terrorists continue to hold other circus performers hostage in their encampments in Las Marías and the jurisdiction of Jucuarán, where their victims are poorly fed, physically abused and forced to sleep on the ground huddled together. Among the captives is José Eugenio Cartagena, owner of the Blanquita circus and uncle of the young clown who managed to escape.

The young getaways also revealed that the terrorists who captured them regularly held diabolic rituals at night, including invocations of Satan, the Magnetic Stone, and the Dark Spirit of the Night, as well as other practices forbidden by our holy Catholic faith.

The two young people are now being well-protected by the Arce Battalion; they have been provided with good-quality clothes and shoes and are presently receiving excellent nourishment to help them recover the strength they lost during their captivity.

Moreover, the information disclosed by the two youngsters is of great importance to the Armed Forces, according to a communiqué issued by a military spokesman.

Finally, it has been disclosed that, in spite of their tender ages, the "little clown" and the dancer Patricia have been living together as man and wife for the past two years and are the parents of a baby daughter, whose whereabouts is unknown to them, but who they assume has also been kidnapped by another group of subversives.

From very early in the morning, the shadow of the pilaster supporting the southeast angle of the roof of the house across the street was longer than usual. The sun's first rays were just beginning to shine, weak and fleeting. Behind the banisters of the heavy balustrade, its paint now flaking from rain and time, familiar shadows began to appear, to be joined later by a file of other silhouettes whose novel clothing set them apart. Outlandish, perhaps, especially in view of what was customary. Above all for someone who had been observing the first movements of the day for many months now. As the years go by, dreams turn to fragile, frightened matter. That's why the dawn is so anxiously awaited and the first light of day gives such a feeling of calm. Brightness that reveals space: corridors, a series of door-ways, windows with grilles, rooms, columns, kiosks, movie billboards that stand out like black bands against the clarity of the street.

They were walking in a tumult. A riot was starting on the corner: people running about, yelling to each other, waving their arms, swirling around the empty stalls of the ladies selling soft drinks. At times, the crowd in the middle of the plaza suddenly shifted towards the centre of the main street to be able to see close up, to satisfy their curiosity. The first mortars had begun to explode just a few minutes before. One on the police station. Another on the National

Guard headquarters. The kids had entered the town as warily as the stealthy shadows of night that disappeared amid the first light of dawn and the crowing of roosters. Taking up key positions, the bulk of them waited till their commandos in charge of storming the Guard and National Police buildings had carried out their missions. Resistance turned out to be light. The commander of the Guard was off whoring. The attack caught him unawares in Juana Puñales' brothel, and the little man was displayed in his underwear right there in the middle of the street, along with the rest of the prisoners.

When the explosions began, no one knew whether it was an act of God, the devil or the kids. The *pum-pum-pum* of the guerrillas' firing spread all over town. People ran recklessly from their houses, then crept forward stealthily, as if part of a dance. On tiptoe along the streets. The sidewalks. Past the billboards advertising movies. Under the shining letters. Next to the rows of newspapers. Across the road. All in the same direction. Down a narrow street with large houses. Till they came to a passageway between two high buildings with wrinkled, discoloured walls full of greasy stains and shreds of layers of political posters that had been pasted up and torn down. Rain and sun, together with children's scribblings, had combined to form a mural with a thick, furrowed surface covered with traces of letters. Numbers. The grotesque, yellowing faces of candidates. Phallic doodles. Phrases. Finally the people went down towards a large esplanade where a crowd was gathering. Children playing. In the background a string of mountains like udders. Full. Another blotch of people on the patio of the mayor's office. And another in the church courtyard. People everywhere. "The kids have taken over the town," they were saying. Always in an impersonal tone.

The kids (and there were a lot of them—girls too)

were young, so young that they looked as though they'd never even fired a gun. But what a sight. Judging from their muddy, muck-filled shoes, they'd come across the river. Afterwards many people emerged from their homes. Listening to the murmur and the same silence that preceded the first explosions. Some left because they had to. Others were simply curious. Little by little, a throng began to form. Now they could look at the kids up close for the first time. Their clothing, their gear. It was not at all exotic. It was, in fact, in a pitiful state: worn-out shoes, pants "a size too big for the deceased". And above all, their weapons: old, parts soldered together, patched up with some used truck part fitted by an ingenious tinsmith. People continued arriving from every corner of the town—more of them all the time. It was turning into a fiesta. The kids' prisoners were targets of joking irony. Wolves and ogres in the power of Tom Thumbs and Little Red Riding Hoods. "The kids have taken over the town," people kept saying.

Other townsfolk came down from the market, bringing bread, flowers, empanadas, coffee, and sweets "for the kids". "*La Prensa* calls them 'terrorists,'" said the bus dispatcher. "But who the hell believes *La Prensa* any more?" he answered himself. The students showed up, fooling around as always, causing a commotion. Touching each other. The girls wearing make-up and looking saucy. "It seems like Carnival," said the fat guy from the Bar Berlín.

During those hours—which were centuries—promises of love were exchanged. New dreams invented. New alliances made. Many people awoke from a prolonged lethargy. Others died when they looked in the mirror. Everybody knew, though, that the whole thing couldn't last. Felt the premonition of danger. A sickening stench began to float in from the distance, clinging to the houses and streets. Rumours arrived. Warnings. Noises like rocks being dragged along by a tumultuous river. The kids felt the town was in danger of turning into a trap. To forestall it, they started out—with provisions and prisoners—on the trip back. At that moment the bells of the Church of Our Lady began to toll, though the echo was lost amid the din. "They say that the kids have taken over the town," people said.

Suddenly everyone stared up at the sky. Then scattered, running down the street. Looking for shelter. Crowds of people scurrying like ants looking for their anthill.

"The Germans are coming!" one boy yelled to another as they ran.

"You idiot!" the other shouted back, playing at war. "Those aren't Germans. They're Americans, and they're gonna drop the atom bomb on us!"

Seconds later three helicopters flew over the town. Coming in low, almost scraping the roofs and treetops. Disappearing around the church towers and then suddenly doubling back again just over the palm trees.

Bombs began falling one after another. One after another. Another. There was a huge explosion. A bomb fell on the bell tower. The vibration travelled through the walls of the houses. Windows banged shut, showering shards of glass. Everything shattered inside the rooms: not a single plate, glass, mirror, frame or windowpane remained intact. The blast twisted everything in its path: chairs, balconies, masonry, telephone poles, antennas, refrigerators, chests of drawers. Another bomb ripped through the black diagram of the municipal sewer system. Fragments of water pipe were embedded in the walls, and a filthy, metallic liquid gushed from the broken mains and oozed into the street.

People ran about inside their houses, amid voices,

shouts, the screams of children. Dazed by the explosions, running amid burning clothing, corpses. Amid crushed medicine bottles, tins of cooking oil, cans of juice, sauces, macaroni, clams. Everything blown out of its container. People were still running. They hid under eves, on street corners, and then kept going, directionless, running over broken glass, ironwork, bricks.

Not a stone was left standing.

Other shadows are outlined now by the banisters of the heavy balustrade. Torn images. The dead, the wounded, debris. The dead. Difficult to count up. So many of them. And there would have been more if the kids hadn't pulled back. If I'm alive today, it's a total miracle. Maybe. Possibly. To tell the story.